CRASH
LANDING

Written by Becca Davies
Illustrated by Emma McCann
Designed by Alyssa Peacock
Edited by Pat Hegarty

Created by WizzBook Ltd.

First published in the UK
by Potter Books, RH17 5PA, UK

www.potterbooks.co.uk

Printed in the UK by CPI Bookmarque, Croydon, CR0 4TD

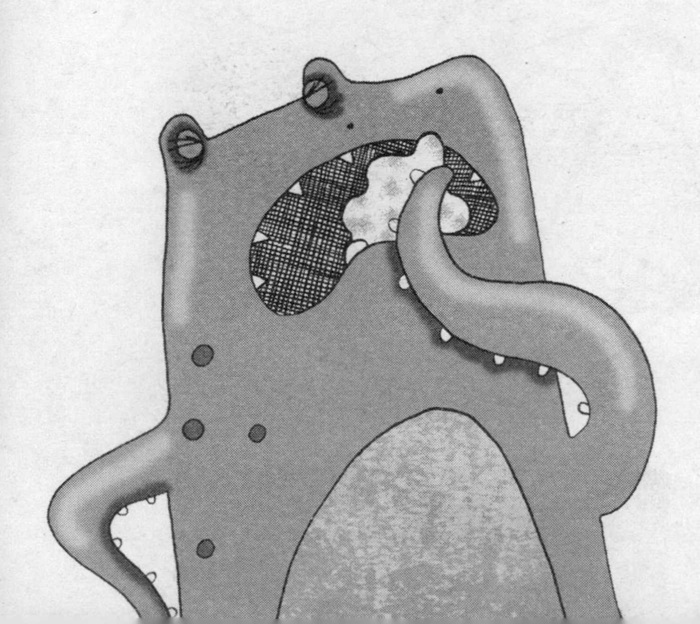

Becca Davies
Illustrated by Emma McCann

CHAPTER 1

The pirate ship, Comet, a creaky old galleon with tattered sails, went soaring through the starry sky, spinning wildly as it hurtled towards the ground. High in the sky was not the usual place for a pirate ship to be, and when it hit there was going to be the most tremendous crash.

C R R R R U U U U N N N C C H H!

Oliver and Becky had eaten their sausage supper and changed into their pyjamas, when their puppy, Scrappy, ran over to the front door and started yapping madly at the top of his voice.

"What was that?" cried Becky, dashing to the window to look outside.

"I don't know," said Oliver, "but we'd better find out. Dad's snoring away in front of the TV, and if the noise wakes him up it'll be straight to bed for us."

But as soon as they opened the door, Scrappy made a run for it!

The little dog ran down the garden towards the big, dark, broken-down shape that had certainly not been there that afternoon. Before they could catch him, he ran up the gangplank and on to what looked for all the world like an old-fashioned pirate ship. Oliver and Becky crept after him, their eyes wide.

As soon as they had clambered on board, Oliver and Becky found themselves inside a dark, rather smelly cabin, surrounded by ferocious-looking men, some with eye-patches, some with wooden legs, and all of them looking very scary indeed.

Becky's knees went wobbly and her voice went squeaky. "Who are you?" she asked. "And where did you come from?"

Oliver pushed his little sister behind him. "They're pirates!" he shouted. "Black-hearted, dirty, double-crossing pirates!" The pirates looked at one another.

"I think that's a bit mean," grumbled one of them, a great big bear of a man whose face was nearly hidden in his enormous, bushy beard.

"I don't think we're black-hearted," another ventured. He was a skinny, grinning

man with a gold tooth and stripy silk trousers. He had a patch over one eye and looked distinctly grubby behind the ears.

"Your fingernails are black, Captain," said another, smaller pirate. "And we're quite dirty, Captain, that's true. You haven't changed your underpants for weeks."

The Captain looked sulky. "Well we're not double-crossers, anyway," he growled. "Except for you, Lofty Left-Eye. You cheat at tiddlywinks."

"It's true," agreed Lofty cheerfully. "I do cheat at tiddlywinks. Captain Flavius Flynn here doesn't change his underpants as often as he should and Brutus there tends to pick his nose and burp after meals. But really we're just lost. Maybe you can help?"

"Lost?" said Oliver. "I should think you are. We're miles and miles from the sea."

The stripy-trousered pirate, the one called Captain Flynn, shrugged his shoulders. "We're Star Pirates. We sail the Seven Solar Systems, looking for treasure. Arrrrr."

Becky and Oliver goggled at the pirates, then at each other, then back at the pirates again. Oliver shrugged. "Arrrrr," he said.

CHAPTER 2

"We've been all over the universe!" said Captain Flynn.

"Arrrrr," agreed Lofty Left-Eye. "Last week it was my turn to be captain. We went to a planet that was nothing but sea, and had a mighty battle with a ferocious space-whale. Cook's still making the leftovers into sandwiches, aren't you, Cook?"

A very fat pirate nodded and grinned. His apron was caked in all sorts of ghastly who-knows-what, and Becky didn't think she'd

MUM
Jam
Space-
whale
Jam

want him to cook for her unless he'd washed his hands first. And possibly burned his apron. "Space-whale pies!" he said. "Space-whale jam and space-whale jelly!" His smile faded a bit as he went on. "Space-whale on toast and space-whale nuggets. I'm awfully tired of space-whale."

"Arrrrr," moaned Brutus. "What I wouldn't give for a nice sausage, or a sticky bun."

"Anything but space-whale," agreed the other pirates.

"Anyway," interrupted Lofty as Cook sat down on a handy barrel, looking glum, "This week it's Flavius Flynn's turn to captain the ship." He leaned closer to the children, who leaned back. Lofty smelled exactly like someone who'd been living on old space-whale for a week. "Old Flavius is a good sort," he confided, "but he's really rubbish at steering."

"Hey!" said Captain Flynn in a hurt voice. "How am I supposed to know what you mean by 'hard astern' and 'port' this and 'starboard' that? Why can't you just say, "turn the pointy end that way" like any normal person?"

Lofty patted him consolingly on the shoulder. "It's not very piratey, Captain," he explained.

"Anyway," sulked Captain Flynn. "It's not my fault the Scrofulons stole our map.

Howling Jack's the man to blame." There was a sudden yelp from the back of the group of pirates, and a thin, trembling man with a peg-leg jumped a foot in the air and launched himself head-first into a barrel, with a loud crash.

The pirates rolled their eyes and hauled their skinny shipmate out with a lot of confusion and bumping into one another. Brutus patted him on the shoulder with one huge, paw-like hand, making him stagger. "This here is Howling Jack," he said. He lowered his voice. "A fine pirate, and he climbs like a monkey, but a terrible coward."

Howling Jack was shaking so hard he could hardly speak. "It's t-t-true," he said. "I am a coward. And I'm scared of the Scrofulons." He tried to bolt for his barrel, but Brutus caught him by the back of his trousers and stopped him.

"What are the Scrofulons?" asked Oliver.

Howling Jack's knees knocked together and he clutched at Brutus's sleeve. "They're great gruesome green aliens!" he wailed. "They've stolen our map, and they're going to steal our treasure, and for all I know they want to eat us for lunch, gobble-crunch!"

Brutus patted him absent-mindedly on the back. "It would make a change," he said thoughtfully, "from space-whale."

CHAPTER 3

SOMETHING SMELLS FISHY

Flavius Flynn looked stern. "It's no use, Howling Jack," he said. "We know all your hiding places. Up in the crow's nest. Out on the poop deck..."

"Once I found him squashed into a cannon," said Lofty Left-Eye.

"But you lost the map, and you'll have to come with us to get it back."

Howling Jack's bottom lip stuck out so far that the parrot tried to perch on it.

He flapped frantically at the parrot, and

the parrot went crackers. By the time Brutus had grabbed Howling Jack by the scruff of the neck and Cook had grabbed the parrot by the tail feathers and threatened to throw him in the stew pot, everything was covered in red and blue feathers and everyone was feeling bad-tempered.

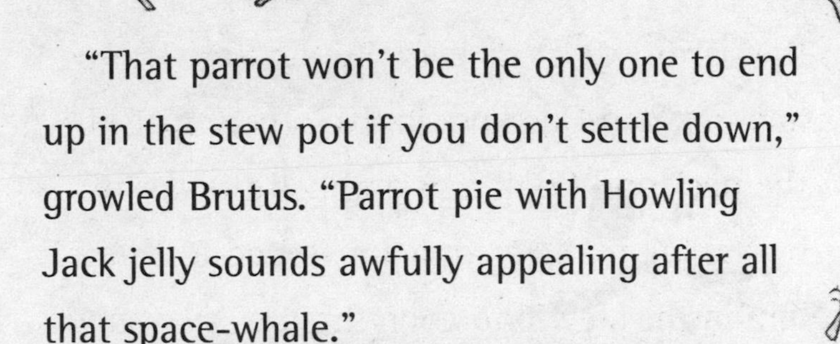

“That parrot won’t be the only one to end up in the stew pot if you don’t settle down,” growled Brutus. “Parrot pie with Howling Jack jelly sounds awfully appealing after all that space-whale.”

There was a bit of sulky muttering from Jack, and a rude-sounding croak from the parrot, but after a while everyone had settled down enough for Oliver to ask, “So how did the Scrofulons get the map in the first place?”

“It was a wicked plot,” said Lofty Left-Eye. “A cunning and desperate ruse. It all started when a visitor came calling for Cook.”

“A boat came alongside,” said Cook.

“And a fellow asked to come aboard, saying he was a sausage-seller. He had a great long coat and a hat pulled down over his eyes.

"Well, at that time we'd have given anything for a sausage, but something smelled fishy to me." He tapped his nose.

"Probably the space-whale," muttered Howling Jack under his breath.

"Anyway," continued Cook with a glare, "I sent him on his way."

Flavius Flynn took up the story. "Next day, this letter was slipped through the porthole."

He fumbled in his filthy shirt and passed a crumpled piece of paper to Oliver.

Oliver looked at the paper. The message was made out of letters that had been cut, not very neatly, out of a newspaper. "Give us the map, or the parrot gets it," he read.

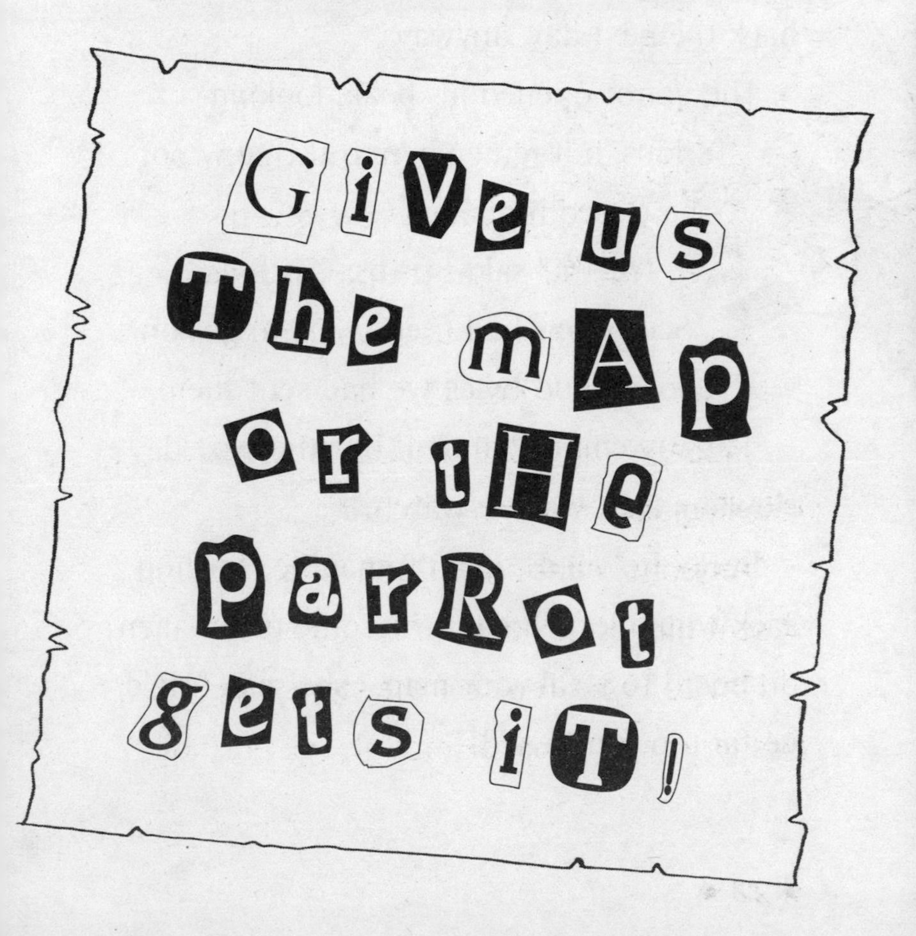

"I saw through their fiendish trickery at once," said Flavius Flynn, "and I folded the paper up to put under a wobbly table leg, so thwarting their evil plans."

"He can't read," confided Lofty Left-Eye. "We were lucky there. And the parrot came back the next day, anyway."

The parrot opened his beak, looking furious, but remembering the stew pot, he closed it again.

"Arrrrr," said Brutus. "So those Scrofulons had tried twice to get on board, and twice we had sent them away empty-handed. But the next day Howling Jack was on watch."

Becky frowned. "I can't imagine Howling Jack would let a great, gruesome green alien on board to steal your map," she said. "He'd be far too frightened!"

"It tricked me," sulked Howling Jack. "It would have fooled anyone."

The other pirates howled with laughter. "A Scrofulon..." sniggered Lofty.

"In a dress..." chortled Flavius Flynn.

"Carrying a handbag and talking in a squeaky voice..." snorted Mr Bones.

"And Howling Jack thought it was his mother!" Cook fell over and kicked his chubby legs in the air, clutching at his big fat belly, helpless with laughter.

"Could've been my mother," grumbled Howling Jack, as the other pirates wiped their eyes and stifled giggles.

"It said it was really proud I'd grown up into such a brave and handsome swashbuckling pirate."

"That should have been a clue, right there," Brutus pointed out. "You've got a face like a moon-dragon's bottom. And brave? Why, every time you even hear the word 'Scrofulon' you dive for your barrel."

Howling Jack, true to form, dived for his barrel.

CHAPTER 4

Brutus sighed through his beard. "Well you needn't worry, Howling Jack," he said. "The Comet has a hole in her hull that's the size of your head. We'll not be sailing to save our plunder from the scurvy Scrofulons any time soon." The pirates nodded gloomily.

"Well you certainly can't stay here!" squawked Oliver.

"Dad'll go mad!" cried Becky. "We had to nag him and nag him before he let us get a puppy. He'll never let us keep a pirate crew in the back garden!"

Suddenly, Oliver had a brainwave. "Wait here!" he said, and with that he disappeared down the gangplank and ran up the garden towards the house.

The pirates fidgeted. Visits from small girls weren't something they were used to. They were good at waving their cutlasses around and blood-curdling screams, but they had a feeling this

wasn't the time for that sort of thing.

"Er...would you like a cup of tea and a biscuit?" rumbled Brutus, scratching his beard.

Cook came through from the kitchen with a huge metal pot. "Ship's biscuits are all full of maggots," he said. "It's grog to drink, and space-whale surprise."

"*I'm* not surprised," said Lofty Left-Eye.

Becky sat down nervously as Flavius slopped a big helping of raw space-whale on to her plate. It was wobbly and slimy, and looked like it had

tentacles in it. “I find it quite surprising,” Becky admitted. She poked a greyish lump with her fork, which bounced off with a booiiooiiooing noise. She wondered if pirates who didn’t eat their dinner were made to walk the plank.

Just then, she was rescued from having to actually taste the vile glop when Oliver dashed back up the gangplank with a big wooden board under his arm. He plonked the board down on the floor. “We can use this to repair the hole in the ship!” he said.

“It’s your electric train set!” said Becky.

Sure enough, the board had little railway tracks running around it. Oliver put some model trains down on the floor next to it.

"Right!" A big, scarred pirate pushed his way to the front of the group. "Mr Bones, ship's surgeon, at your service. I also do the carpentry. Comes in handy when I'm fitting wooden legs." He waved a hammer at the surprised children.

Sitting on Mr Bones' shoulder was a little green creature that was squeaking and squelching and dribbling slime.

"And this here is Squit, my loyal assistant. He passes me tools and helps with the bandages and the fiddly bits. I used to have a parrot, but it was no good at tying knots."

On the other side of the cabin, a brightly coloured parrot ruffled its feathers grumpily and gave a squawk that sounded remarkably like a rude word.

Squit squeaked happily, stretched out a tentacle and grabbed a bunch of big nails from a pocket in Mr Bones' tool belt.

"Stand back, me hearties, and we'll soon have her underway!"

CHAPTER 5

Mr Bones nailed the train set board into place over the hole in the bottom of the ship. As soon as he had finished, the little alien Squit starting arranging toy trains on the tracks and burbling happily to himself.

"It won't work," said Brutus glumly. "It was a good try, lad, but it's not just the hole. The power's gone as well. The rocket boosters won't fire – we'll never get the Comet airborne."

Squit took no notice of the gloomy crew.

Taking a tentacle full of wires from the board, he tied them into a complicated knot, chirping and squelching happily.

"Arrrrr," agreed Cook. "And it'll be cold space-whale for breakfast, lunch and dinner." The pirates groaned.

Squit pushed the bundle of wires through a hole in the ship's planks. Then he reached across and flipped a lever on the train set board. Immediately, the little trains started trundling around the tracks. At the same time, all the lamps in the cabin came on in a blaze of light, and Oliver and Becky heard a loud whooshing noise. They lurched forward as the Comet shuddered into the sky.

"The rockets are firing!" said Mr Bones, as all the pirates grinned from ear to ear. "Well done, Squit – we're off to the stars!"

Oliver was beside himself with excitement. "Don't you mean the stARRRRRs?" he said.

All the pirates glared at him.

"Er, it was a joke," he said. "You see, pirates say... "

"We know," growled Flavius Flynn. "We've heard it. And the one about the wooden leg.

And the one about the giant squid... "

"And that one isn't even true," added Lofty quickly. "None of us would do a disgusting thing like that. And anyway, we promised never to talk about it."

Brutus threw his arm around Oliver's shoulders. "The jokes get you down after a while," he said. "But it's a good life, sailing the Seven Solar Systems. Why, we've seen planets made entirely of gold... "

"We've *stolen* planets made entirely of gold," said Flavius, his gold tooth flashing.

"Not stolen, not stolen," corrected Brutus. "Plundered. It's a perfectly respectable piratey activity. We've seen planets with all the moons tied on with string so the people could climb up and down. We've seen some fabulous treasures and horrible monsters..." He hesitated, and then went on. "But we've never come up against anything quite as horrible as the Scrofulons." He paused to think. "Except perhaps the giant squid."

Lofty Left-Eye scowled. "We said we wouldn't talk about the giant squid!"

CHAPTER 6

Oliver and Becky gaped as they saw the Earth fall away behind them, looking no bigger than a marble, smeared blue and green and floating in the vastness of space. Becky suddenly felt very homesick indeed.

But Oliver's eyes were shining with excitement as he peered out of the porthole.

"It's an adventure, Becky. A real, honest-to-goodness adventure." He put his arm around his sister. "Just think of all the things we could see. Look out there!" He pointed.

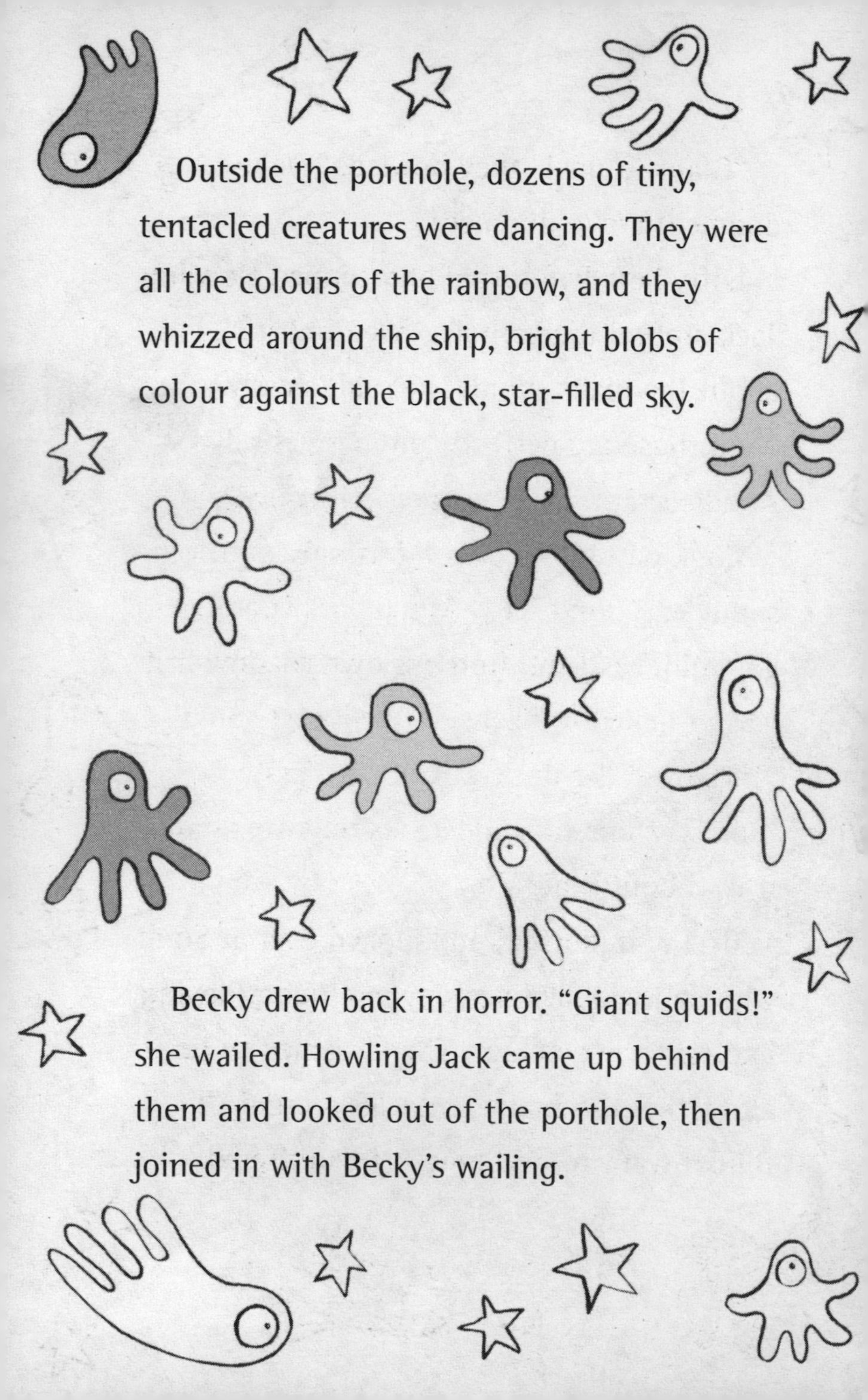

Outside the porthole, dozens of tiny, tentacled creatures were dancing. They were all the colours of the rainbow, and they whizzed around the ship, bright blobs of colour against the black, star-filled sky.

Becky drew back in horror. “Giant squids!” she wailed. Howling Jack came up behind them and looked out of the porthole, then joined in with Becky’s wailing.

"Giant squids!" they howled. "We're doomed! We're doomed!"

Lofty Left-Eye tutted and clipped Howling Jack around the earhole. "We don't talk about the giant squid!" he said, crossly. "And those are perfectly ordinary astral squidlets, Jack, as you very well know."

Cook patted Becky comfortingly on the shoulder. "Don't let Howling Jack spook you, girl. He'd run from his own shadow if it wasn't nailed to his heels. We'll cast some lines from the deck, and yer old mate Cook'll make some delicious tentacle stew. How about that?"

Becky shuddered, and looked over at Squit who had wrapped Scrappy in a gooey, loving and tentacly embrace. There seemed to be altogether too many tentacles around. "I think I want to go home," she muttered.

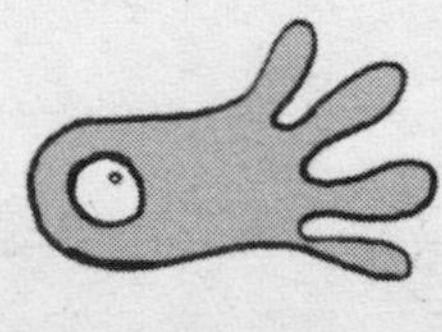

But now Oliver was whispering intently with Captain Flynn. The Captain grinned his gold-toothed grin and turned to the rest of the crew. “Planet ahoy!” he yelled cheerfully. “Off the pointy end! Finish your grog and fetch your cutlasses, we’re landing on Scrofulon Prime to take back our treasure map!”

Scrofulon Prime was a great warty green planetoid surrounded by a murky fog that swirled and boiled like unappetising soup – maybe even tentacle stew. Even from the cabin, Oliver and Becky could smell its stink of rotten eggs and boiled cabbage.

As the pirates ran around, yelling and fighting, Brutus took Howling Jack firmly by the collar, Oliver took Becky's hand and they all took deep breaths. Bumpety-bump! The Comet touched down on Scrofulon Prime.

CHAPTER 7

They stepped off the Comet and into thick, stinking ooze that sucked at their feet and tried to eat their shoes. There was a weird hush, and they all found themselves moving closer together. Brutus snuffled and wiped his nose on his sleeve – slurrrrrp.

"Shhhh," said Oliver. "We don't know what's out there." The pirates pressed closer together still, until they looked like one big creature with lots of legs that had got its clothes out of a dustbin and badly needed a bath. The smell and the muck on the planet's surface made even the Comet's scurvy crew think longingly of soap and hot water. Howling Jack was right in the middle of the group, trembling so hard that the whole crew looked like it was vibrating.

Squit waved his tentacles in agitation. He tried to climb up Becky's leg, clinging on and closing his eyes tight, but Becky gave a tiny squeak, hopping around in fright and trying to shake the little creature off.

"Shhhh!" said Oliver, crossly. "We have to be quiet. This could be dangerous!" He pulled Squit off his sister and held the little alien in his arms, where he put his tentacles over his eyes. Scrappy trotted along behind them.

Carefully, they set off through the swamp, trying not to take deep breaths of the rancid air, fighting the ooze at every step.

Then, in the mist, they heard a noise.

Slurrrrrrrrrrrrrrrrrrrrrrrrrrrpppp.

"Brutus!" snapped Flavius Flynn. "The lad's told you to be quiet. Now keep it down, you scurvy dog!"

"Um, Captain..." said Brutus.

"Hush!" chorused the pirates.

"But, Captain..."

"What is it?" whispered Oliver, exasperated.

"That wasn't me!" said Brutus.

"Then who was it?" snapped Oliver.

Howling Jack gulped. "I think..." he said, slowly, pointing a trembling finger, "I think it was them."

As the mist cleared, the pirates stared. All around them were dozens of aliens, huge and horrible with oozing, squashy bodies. Looking like a cross between a fat, warty toad and a slippery, slimy octopus, they sat in the murk making revolting belching, squelching noises.

"Gentlemen," said one, and there was a

gust of foul breath and a glimpse of huge, sharp teeth, "Welcome to Scrofulon Prime."

That was when they knew they were in real trouble. He had called the crew of the Comet 'gentlemen'. Anyone who could tell a lie that big was bad news. And then he laughed – a horrible, wet, snorting sound – as his fellow Scrofulons led the pirates away.

CHAPTER 8

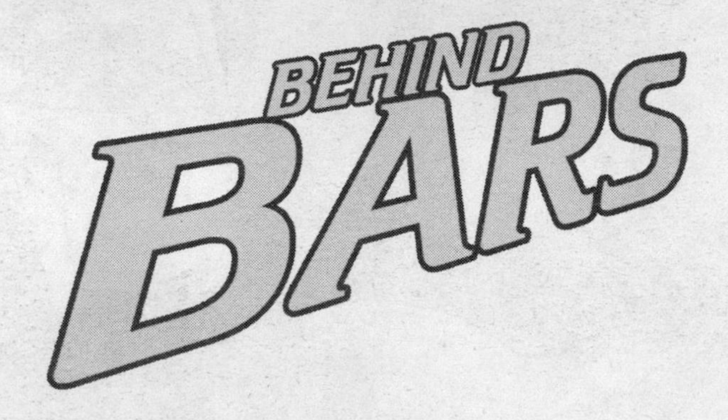

Oliver, Becky and the pirate crew sat and stared unhappily at the bars of their cell. Their very small cell. Five pirates, two children, a puppy and a small green alien were squashed together with heads stuck in armpits and feet wedged uncomfortably under bottoms. Flavius Flynn's seldom-changed underpants were, at such close quarters, frankly whiffy. Unspeakable green ooze dripped from the ceiling. Oliver could feel a big blob of it dribbling down his neck.

After a while, Brutus spoke. "I could dress up as an old lady," he rumbled. "I could trick the guards into letting us out."

There was a thoughtful silence. Everyone looked at Brutus, with his enormous bushy beard (especially Oliver, who was squashed into a position where he could see right up the big pirate's nose). "No..." he said, trying not to imagine Brutus in a frock. "I don't think that would work. Anyway, there aren't any guards. Just some very strong bars and a great big lock."

Everyone fell silent again, then all of a sudden, five pirate voices began to talk at once, at the tops of their voices and at cross-purposes...

"We could dig a tunnel with the Captain's gold tooth!"

"We could bake a cake with a file in it!"

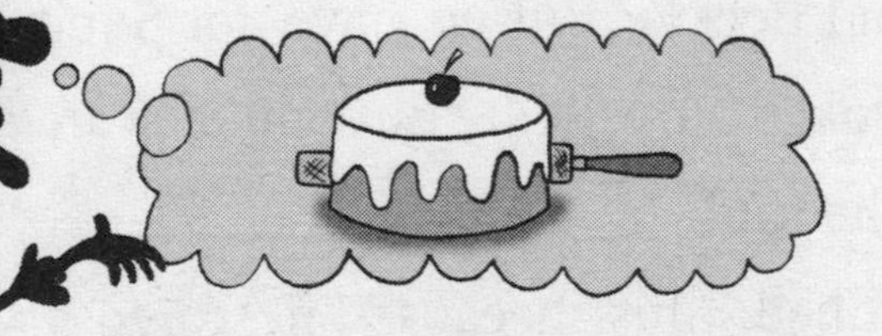

"...a really strict diet, and slip between the bars..."

"...train a monkey to bring us the key..."

"Shut up, shut up, shut up!" Oliver shouted so loudly that the pirates were shocked into silence. "It's hopeless. We're stuck. We haven't got a cake with a file in it. I can't see you in a dress, Brutus. And we haven't got a trained monkey."

"No," said Becky. "But we have got Squit."

Oliver looked surprised. "But you're scared of Squit," he said.

Becky sighed. "Just because I'm scared doesn't mean I'm stupid," she said. "I've seen him squash himself up and stretch and..." she shuddered, "...ooze. He can squeeze through the bars and bring us the key hanging on that wall over there."

Oliver and the pirates gaped first at her, and then at the key that they had been too busy arguing about to notice.

Squit practically purred with pleasure. No sooner had Becky finished speaking than he oozed over to the bars, wriggled and squiggled his way through, and stretched a tentacle up, up, up, to unhook a rusty key from the wall opposite the pirates' cell.

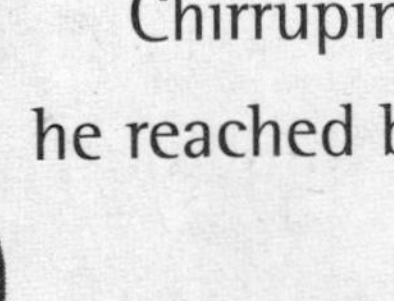

Chirruping, he reached back

through the bars and proudly held the key out to Becky. She took it cautiously between her thumb and forefinger, trying to ignore the fact that it was now unpleasantly sticky.

"Thank you, Squit," she said in as friendly a voice as she could manage, and passed the key quickly to Oliver before wiping her fingers on her pyjamas. Oliver's mouth was still open.

"That was amazing, Becky!" he said.

"I know," said Becky, smiling.

"Now let's get out of here! It's a bit too underpanty and armpitty in here." Click. Oliver turned the key, and the door to the cell swung open with a creak.

CHAPTER 9

SQUELCHING SCROFULONS

The corridor outside the cell was dim, damp and clammy. Pirates, pets and children picked themselves up off the floor, and patted themselves to make sure all their bits were still attached and not too bashed about.

"Everyone hush!" said Oliver. "We have to find out where the Scrofulons are – that's where the treasure map will be. And we have to do it quietly. We'll just creep down this corridor..."

"We're not very good at creeping," said Lofty Left-Eye. "Rushing in and screaming, that's more our style."

"Swingin' in on ropes with cutlasses between our teeth," said Brutus.

"Shivering timbers and swashing buckles. Rampaging and roaring," said Flavius Flynn.

Lofty Left-Eye saw how cross Oliver looked. "But this time we'll be as quiet as little mice," he said. "Titchy, tiny little mice, scampering on their little pink feet."

Secretly, Oliver thought they probably would be as quiet as mice – if mice wore big boots and shouted a lot. But they'd have to do the best they could.

Howling Jack said nothing. He couldn't decide what frightened him most – what lay ahead, or what might be behind them – so he was trying to see in all directions at once.

As a result, he was spinning round and round on the spot, and whimpering.

Oliver sighed. "Just do your best," he said. "And stop that, Howling Jack, you'll make yourself dizzy. Now, which way should we go?"

Brutus picked his nose thoughtfully and looked around him.

"There's a trail of slime on the floor here," he said. He snorted and snuffled into his sleeve. Brutus was a man with a lot of experience of slime.

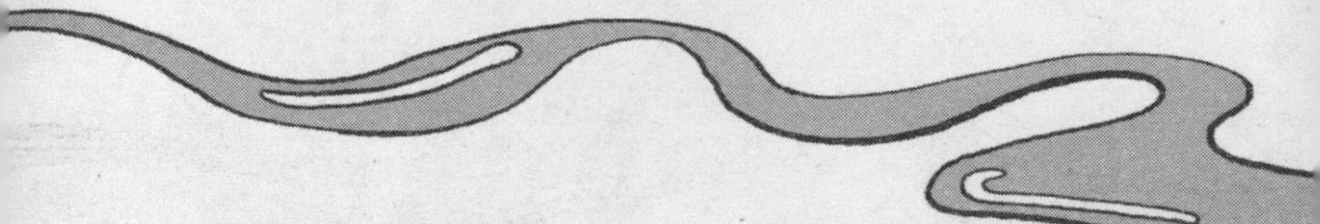

“I reckon,” he said, “if we follow it, we’ll get to where the Scrofulons are.”

“Right,” said Oliver. “Let’s go. And...oh, Howling Jack’s fallen over. Pick him up and dust him off, will you Brutus?”

They set off along the sticky trail, bumping into each other, to a chorus of “Shhhh, be quiet!” from Oliver and Becky.

“I still think we should have rushed in screaming,” began Lofty peevishly, but then they heard a noise from ahead of them. A burping, belching, squelching noise, coming from a half-open door.

Oliver turned to his sister. “Stay here and keep this lot quiet,” he said. “I’m going to see what’s in there.” Becky looked pale and a bit sick, but she managed a nod.

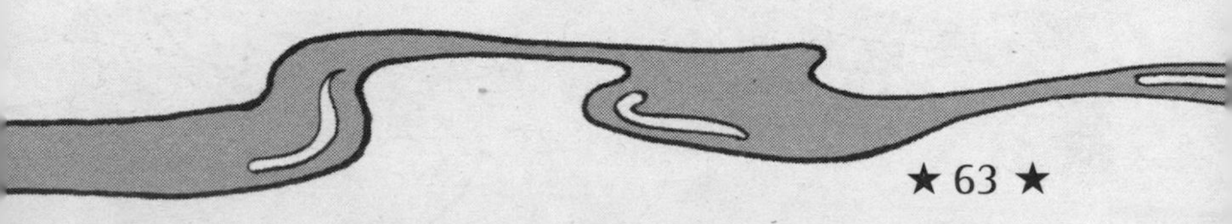

Oliver sneaked over to the door on tip-toes. Holding his breath, he peeped around it. After a few moments he turned back to his friends and beckoned. Becky raised a finger to her lips, reminding the rowdy pirates to be quiet, and they all shuffled over to the door.

Five pirate heads peeped around the door. Five pirate jaws dropped.

Becky's eyes widened, and she gasped.

Beyond the door was an enormous hall, the biggest room any of them had ever seen. At least a hundred Scrofulons were squelching their sticky, smelly way around the stone floor. And there, in the middle of the hall, surrounded by the enemy, was their beloved ship, the Comet.

CHAPTER 10

One by one, they sidled into the great hall.

"What are we going to do now?" whispered Flavius Flynn. "How can I be a pirate captain without a ship? We might as well hand in the peg-legs and the parrot, and get paper rounds."

Mr Bones set his jaw. "I built that ship, every nail and every plank, with these two hands." There was an indignant squeak from Squit. "And half a dozen tentacles, of course. What I've done once I can do again."

Flavius Flynn looked quite tearful. "You're a good man, Mr Bones, and a fine pirate. But even if you could build us another ship, what use would it be without our treasure map? No, we're done for."

"So the important thing is to get the treasure map back?" said Becky thoughtfully.

Flavius Flynn looked at his crew. Brutus was scratching his beard, causing a small avalanche of dandruff, and Lofty's face was screwed up in thought, making him look as if he really needed to go to the toilet. Howling Jack, for some reason, was counting on his fingers and looking confused. But it didn't look as though any of them had a brilliant plan.

"I reckon so," he said hopelessly. He sniffed miserably.

"So if we knew where the treasure map

was, and I could think of a way to get it, then everything would be okay?" Becky said.

"*If* we did...and *if* you could," said Flavius Flynn, his lip wobbling as he tried not to cry.

"That's easy, then," said Becky. "It's on that table over there. Someone just needs to sneak over and get it."

The pirates all turned to look. Sure enough, on a table in the middle of the hall, just in front of the stolen ship, was a curled, yellowing and rather tattered piece of parchment – the pirates' treasure map!

"I don't suppose rushing in and screaming would work in this situation?" said Lofty Left-Eye, hopefully. He saw Becky's expression and answered himself: "No, I suppose not."

"I'll sneak over and get it!" said Oliver. "I'm the smallest, apart from Becky, so they're much less likely to notice me."

"I should go," rumbled Brutus. "I'm the strongest and the best at fighting if they catch me at it."

"Well I'm the captain," said Flavius Flynn, "this week, anyway. I'll go."

But once again, Becky surprised them all.

"Howling Jack should go," she said.

The pirates looked amazed and doubtful – none more so than Howling Jack.

"I know," said Becky. "He's a coward. But that means he's good at sneaking. He spends his life skulking and sidling past anything scary. You, Jack, are our only hope."

So, quivering and shaking so hard that he looked blurred around the edges, Howling Jack set out across the great hall

towards the table. The Scrofulons stood with their backs to it, gloating over their capture of the Comet. Just a few more steps, and the map would be in his hands...

But Howling Jack's nerve failed him. His teeth started to chatter, clickety-clack, and his knees started to knock, clonkety-clonk. The Scrofulons turned, and Howling Jack froze with one hand outstretched to take the map. At that instant, Oliver, Becky and the rest of the crew heard the door slam behind them and the bolt drawn across. The Scrofulons had taken them captive once more.

What happens next... you decide!

This story has two alternative endings and you get to choose the one you like best. If you like the idea of a 'Hideous Monster' saving the day then chapter 11 A is the ending for you.

If you would like to see how the 'Pirates' Treasure' saves their skin, then turn to page 83 for chapter 11 B.

CHAPTER 11 A

The pirates huddled together, while halfway across the room Howling Jack's knees went weak and he crumpled up. "Mummy!" he yelped as he collapsed in a heap on the floor, wobbling like a jelly.

Lofty had leapt into Flavius Flynn's arms, while Oliver and Becky hid behind Brutus, peeping out from either side of the big pirate. Squit had wrapped himself around Mr Bones, who was marching madly about in nervous circles, wild-eyed and muttering to himself, looking like nothing so much as an agitated clockwork soldier.

The only one who didn't seem worried was Scrappy, whose little puppy brain was too small to realise the danger they were in. He lolloped around happily, ears flopping and tail wagging. Then, spotting his new friend Howling Jack across the room, he set off in a bounding run, yapping cheerfully, heading straight towards the Scrofulons.

Suddenly, there was an unearthly screeching noise. The Scrofulons backed away, tentacles waving in horror, cowering back from the puppy.

"What is it?" burbled the fattest of the group. "It's horrible! Keep it away!" There was a weird, bubbling, sobbing noise as the Scrofulons shuffled backwards, looks of disgust and horror on their warty, slimy faces.

"What are they frightened of?" said Oliver. "I don't understand!" Flavius Flynn looked a bit more cheerful. "Is it our fearsome piratical reputation?" he asked hopefully. "They've realised what they're up against at last, I'll wager. They're a-feared of walking the plank!" Becky looked thoughtful. "I don't think so," she said slowly. "I was frightened of Squit because he looked so strange to me.

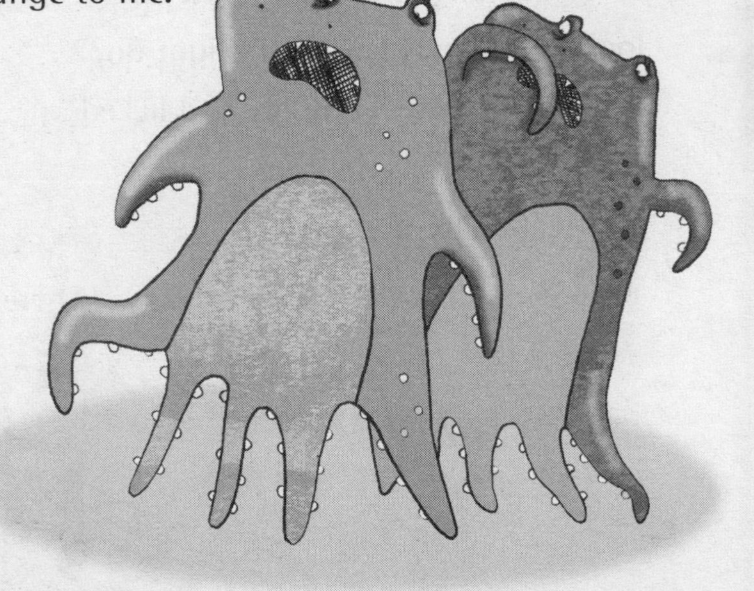

Well, Scrappy must look just as alien to them. They're scared of the puppy!"

Oliver grinned as light dawned. "You're right!" he said. "Here, Scrappy! Here, boy!"

Scrappy scampered back across the room with the daft enthusiasm of all puppies, and Oliver scooped him up and scratched him behind the ears. He grinned. "Listen up, you Scrofulons!" he said. "This is a terrible monster from my home planet. I'm not sure how long I can control it. If it gets loose, who knows what it might do?" Scrappy whined winningly and licked Oliver's face, covering him in affectionate puppy slobber.

"Noooo, please!" wailed the Scrofulons. "It's hideous!" They began to burble and sob, wringing their tentacles, and shuddering and wincing.

"The horrid pointy teeth and all that yelping and yapping!"

"The wagger at the end that thrashes to and fro!" "The fat, fuzzy body and the floppy pink tongue!"

Oliver interrupted, full of confidence now.

"Then I'll take it away on our ship. But only for a price. You must give us back the map and promise not to bother us again."

"Anything!" cried the Scrofulons, "So long as you keep that hideous monster away from us!"

Ten minutes later, they were boarding the Comet. The Scrofulons were full of pathetic gratitude, ushering them on board and grinning nervously. The ceiling of the great hall whirred and drew back like a camera shutter, leaving a hole to the open sky.

“Fire her up, Mr Bones!” said Flavius Flynn. “Splice the mainbrace and unfurl the wotsits. We’re on our way!”

“Wait a minute!” said Becky. “Where’s Howling Jack?”

Then, just as the gangplank was being drawn up, Howling Jack half-leaped, half-scrambled onto the deck of the Comet. Clutched in one grubby hand was the pirates’ treasure map. “I’ve got the map!” he said, waving it triumphantly.

“I saved the day! I saved the day!”

Flavius Flynn opened his mouth to protest that it was Scrappy and Oliver who had saved them, but Becky silenced him with a look. "That's right, Jack," she said. "You're our hero."

The Comet sailed into the starry sky, a battered old galleon in full sail, its rocket boosters flaming orange and red. On board, snoring gently, six happy pirates, two human children, a little green alien and a very tired puppy, headed for Earth. Only a small, bad-tempered parrot peeped out of the porthole, watching the stars go by.

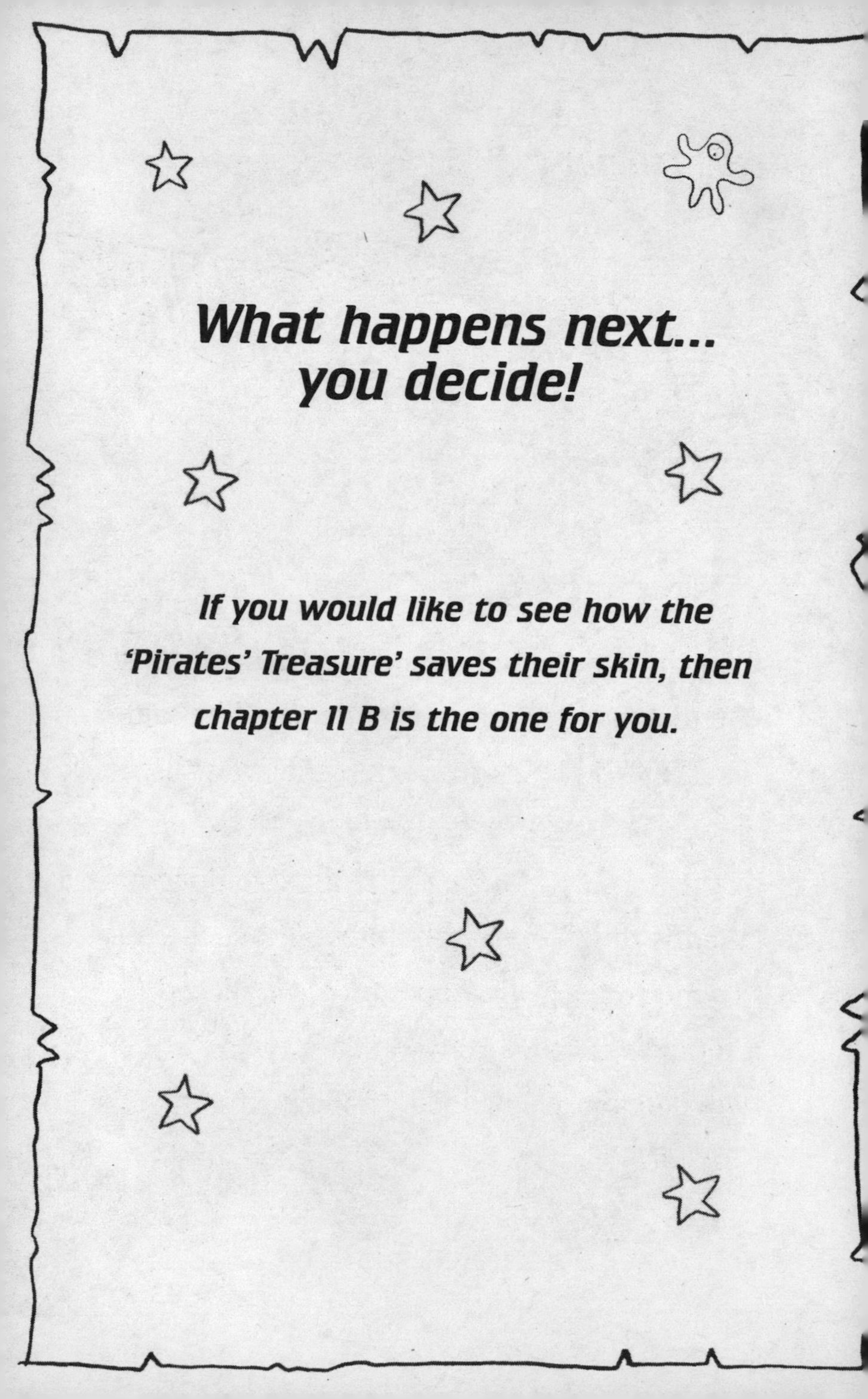

What happens next... you decide!

If you would like to see how the 'Pirates' Treasure' saves their skin, then chapter 11 B is the one for you.

CHAPTER 11 B

A Scrofulon stepped forward. He was bigger than the others, and seemed to be the leader. "Gentlemen, gentlemen, gentlemen," he said. He sounded almost jovial, but that was three big lies in a row! As one man (but not one of them a gentleman), the pirates shuddered. "What's this?" the Scrofulon went on. "Trying to get your map back?" He flicked a tentacle towards Howling Jack, who twitched and whimpered. "Take it," he said. "Take it!"

Howling Jack looked at him with huge eyes, then reached out with trembling fingers to take the creased and grubby map from the table. He clutched it to his chest, still

shaking and wobbling like a pirate-shaped jelly. Groups of Scrofulons were slithering up the gangplank, then sliming back down again, carrying chests and bundles from inside the Comet. They placed them carefully around the big Scrofulon's feet (or where his feet would be if he had feet, rather than tentacles and nodules and odd, slimy bits).

The Scrofulon reached down and flipped back the lid on the biggest chest. A ghastly smell wafted out. Becky put her hand over her nose and mouth. "Yuck!" said Oliver. Even the pirates screwed up their noses and waved their hands in front of their faces.

"You fools!" said the big Scrofulon. "What would we want with your pathetic map, when we already have your treasure – and all the time it was aboard your ship."

He reached a tentacle into the stinking chest, and withdrew a grimy, crumpled bundle. Stuffing it into his mouth, he chewed, rolling his eyes with pleasure

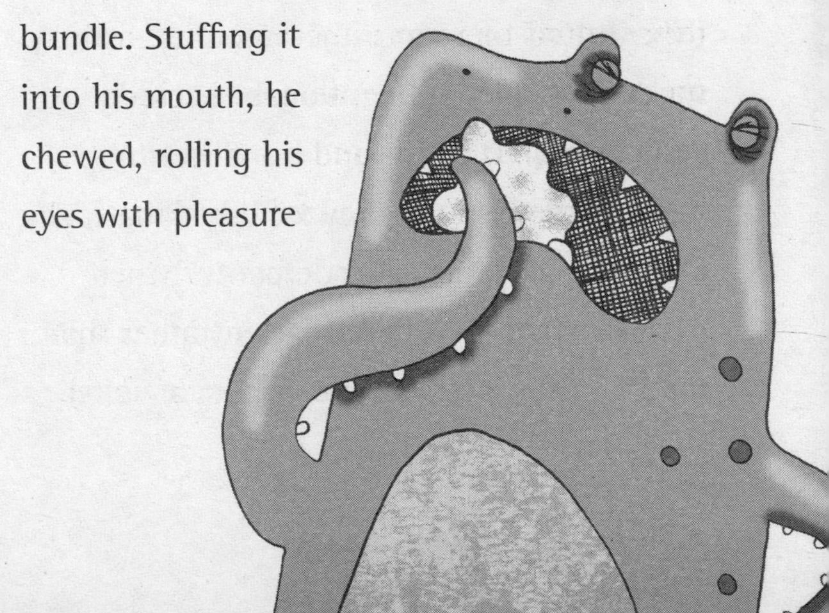

and smacking his chops. Then he patted his stomach and burped loudly. "The finest delicacy in the known universe," he said.

Lofty Left-Eye gasped. "But that's..."

Brutus gaped. "It can't be..."

Oliver was so shocked he sat down hard, with a bump. "Is he eating...?"

Then everybody shouted at once. "It's Flavius Flynn's underpants!"

Sure enough, the Scrofulons had crowded around the boxes and bundles and chests of dirty clothes. With little sighs of pleasure, they stuffed them into their mouths – stinky socks, unwashed unmentionables, crusty vests and all. Oliver found his voice. "And this was the treasure they were looking for? Delicious...nutritious...underpants!"

It was hard to believe that anyone would think of the pirates' dirty washing as

treasure, but before long, with Oliver helping out with the difficult sums, the pirates and the Scrofulons had reached an agreement. The crew of the Comet would supply the Scrofulons with all the stinky underwear they could eat. In return, they would have all the gold they could possibly wish for, and best of all, they were free to leave with their map and ship just as soon as they liked.

At the big Scrofulon's command, the ceiling of the great hall drew back. Five pirates, two children, a little green alien and a puppy scrambled up the gangplank of the Comet. They were greeted by Cook and the happy, raucous shrieks of the parrot, who had even missed Squit. A tiny bit.

"Turn the pointy end towards Earth!" Oliver ordered, happily. Becky smiled, already looking forward to her bed. "Who would have thought," she said, "that anyone would want to eat stinky old underpants?"

"Arrrrr," said Cook. "I can't understand it, myself. Now who's for some delicious space-whale surprise?" The food fight was already well underway as the Comet set sail for planet Earth.

How well do you know the Star Pirates?

1) What do the Star Pirates eat when they are deep in outer space?

a) Space-whale

b) Stinky underpants

c) Squidlets' tentacles

2) Which of these is the Star Pirates' favourite activity?

a) Holding tea parties

b) Plundering whole planets for treasure

c) Walking the plank

3) What type of alien creature does the ship's surgeon have perched on his shoulder?

a) A space parrot

b) A moon-dragon

c) A baby alien octopus

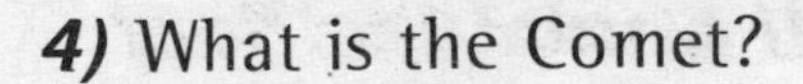

4) What is the Comet?

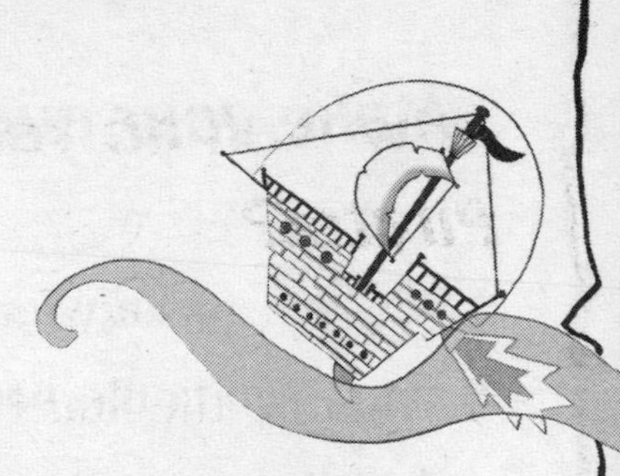

a) A shooting star

b) The Star Pirates' ship

c) An alien planet

5) What are the Scrofulons most afraid of?

a) Puppies

b) Howling Jack getting his hands on the treasure map

c) Squit

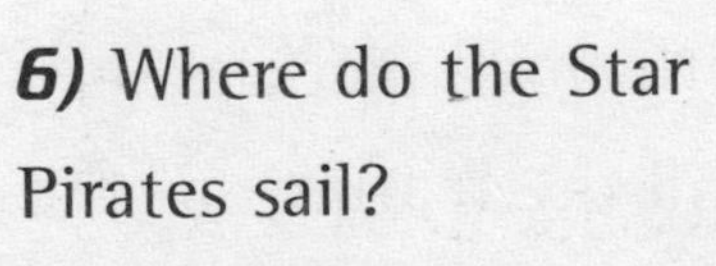

6) Where do the Star Pirates sail?

a) Across the Seven Seas

b) Around the Seven Scrofulon Suns

c) Through the Seven Solar Systems

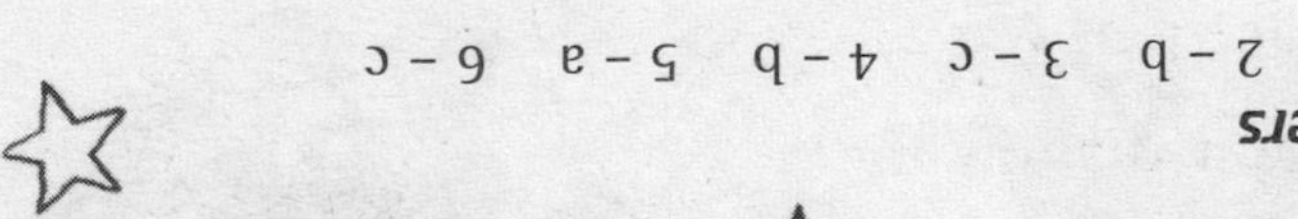

Answers

1 – a 2 – b 3 – c 4 – b 5 – a 6 – c

Make your own treasure map!

Why not make your very own treasure map? You could base it on a planet, an island or even your own back garden.

1) Draw an outline of your chosen place on a piece of paper. Think of a special name for it.

2) Fill in your map with small pictures or symbols to represent all the features of the place you've chosen and colour them in. Use the symbols opposite to help you.

hills

mountains

forest

squidlets

shooting stars

moon caves

Scrofulons

treasure

3) Draw a key explaining what your symbols mean at the top of your map and add a compass in the bottom corner.

4) To make your map look like a real pirate map, press a cold damp tea bag over the page, crumple it up and tear carefully around the edges.

Star tip: Why not use your map for a treasure hunt with your friends? Ask an adult to hide some treasure and some clues for you. The pirate who finds the most treasure wins and gets to be Captain!

How to talk like a pirate...

Here are some essential words and phrases to help you sound just like a Star Pirate!

Arrrrr: a common pirate expression that can be used at almost any time, whatever the situation

Looting: raiding for treasure

Aye: yes

Bilge rat: the bilge is the lowest, yukkiest part of the ship, full of stinky, slimy water. A bilge rat is a very smelly rat that lives in the bilge

Scurvy fellow: a despicable person

Sea rover: a pirate ship

Me hearty: my friend

Avast: stop

Swashbuckling Anagrams!

The Star Pirates have got their words into a bit of a muddle! Can you help untangle the letters below to find some piratey words?

lntaetces **ycusvr rwce**

orfsulcnos

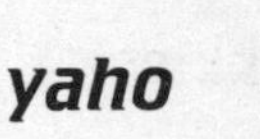

yaho

peacs helwa

elsylm nruaptdnes

itgna dsuiqs

rypcpsa

ltsudiqes

Answers

lntaetces: tentacles, *ycusvr rwce*: scurvy crew, *orfsulcnos*: scrofulons, *yaho*: ahoy, *elsylm nruaptdnes*: smelly underpants, *peacs helwa*: space whale, *itgna dsuiqs*: giant squids, *rypcpsa*: scrappy, *ltsudiqes*: squidlets

In Star Pirates, Solar Circus, the pirate crew embark upon an action-packed mission to rescue their kidnapped crewmate, Brutus, from the non-comical clutches of some crestfallen clowns. Sailing full-speed ahead to the Solar Circus, the Star Pirates explore another corner of the Seven Solar Systems.